IMPErFECT Minds

Paradoxical, mind bending & psychological

I0563098

By Rose Butterfly

A Short Story Collection

Volume 2

May your life be filled
with beautiful stories.

Dear _____

Love & Regards

_____

Have a great time!

Title: Imperfect Minds
eBook/Paperback
ISBN Paperback: 978-0-6452271-7-8
Author: Rose Butterfly
Category: **Short stories/Psychological/Magical Realism**

Cover Design: Deena Philip

Illustrations
Deena Philip
Courtesy: Pixabay

Disclaimer

Author's email: reach2rosebutterfly@gmail.com
team4deen@gmail.com

Contents

STORY #1
LATE NIGHT

Peek a Fear!

If someone were to ever describe me as mischievous or a daredevil, because of my culture, gender and financial disposition; and think that I should be more aware of the world around me and not get lost in the unknown and the mystical element that no one truly comprehends, because they think for a girl like me it poses the possibility of great risk and danger, I would say to them--- 'I wish you would not think of me as a careless or troublesome but rather as an adventurer or a seeker.'

But I am in no capacity to influence what you think, because at the end of the day, I am just a 17-year-old, who clearly did not fit into the usual mould of girls, of the time. The year was 2004.

I was lying down in my bed, looking up at the fan that was spinning at a maximum speed of five, and yet feeling the sweat on my body. I was wearing a red printed kameez and a loose brown bottom. They did not match, and it looked awful on me.

I was that kind of a person who was okay with wearing whatever I could get hold of. More like, choosing a clothing that suited the weather best. This meant ending up with wrong pairs and mismatched clothes often.

Right now, the culprit would be my pyjamas, they were totally out of place for the kameez but were loose and comfy.

My sister would look at me and say, "why can't you pick up a salwar and kameez that match? Why wear such mismatch clothes?'

"Where's the mismatch?" I would ask.

Not that I did not know what was good, I just didn't care much, and so I would look at her big kajal filled eyes and wouldn't know how to respond to all her doubts she had about me and my unconventional ways.

As I was lying there looking at the fan, I could hear my parents talk about other family members, neighbours and the country and then the world in general.

"If we had no greedy politicians, the world would have been heaven." My father said.

"Now, what do we do? When are we going to get the money? When do you think our materials are going to be sold?" My mother asked.

I got up from my bed and walked slowly into the living area.

"What happened, are we short on cash? "I enquired.

"Nothing much to worry about." My father assured with a lack of confidence clearly visible on his face.

"Why not worry Papa?" my sister asked.

"Yes, we are short on cash." She looked at me and said as a matter of fact, like I should have known.

Being the youngest, nobody really told me what was happening in business or at the house. They expected me to eaves drop and understand everything that was going on.

They hesitated to share financial problems and also take money from what I earned, not that I earned much. I performed drama in schools and got paid for it. Just enough to spend on myself.

And sometimes, I got fancy things for the family, like dinner from out, ice creams, new clothes, etc.

My sister was helping father with keeping accounts for 'the business', selling saris. But as a family, I felt that we could do a lot better if we had worked in a thoughtful and more sensible way.

The house, the business, the communication, the food, everything came from a place of simply getting by and nobody wanted anything more.

When I say more, what I mean is that nobody wanted to have fun, take a risk, look at things with a different perspective, talk about a different topic, follow the hearts calling, listen to God, open their eyes and ears to admire the beauty of the world and enjoy life.

The idea of enjoying life, or truly experiencing it, was absent. My parents were of the opinion that it was a waste of time for people like us. They did not think it was meant for simple minded people or middle-class folks.

Interesting topics for discussion, leisure and fun were all reserved for someone else, mostly the rich and not us.

"Instead of wasting your money buying unwanted things, give it to father." My sister said.

"Sure, wait till you see what I got for you." I said, not understanding why anyone had a problem with what I bought.

My mother followed me when I went inside.

"Darling, my dear, it's really good that you are sharing with family. It's a great virtue. It's being kind. You are a good girl." She looked at me lovingly and said those words, which actually did not make much sense to me. Obviously, she would not have thought of it that way.

The reason is because she can change her 'good girl' opinion about anybody at any time and it's a flimsy one that changed too quickly at the slightest unapproved act.

The 'good girl' approval from mother, don't we all care about that tag? But I realised that I had to care a little less about it if I wanted to follow my heart.

It is not possible to make a mother happy and also follow your heart.

Now, if I remember correctly, she had scolded me the other day for behaving badly to her friend. She said to me, "You are a stupid girl, with a lot of clay in your head. All colourful clays that make you see the world in your own way, not listening to anybody."

If you remove the word stupid from it and analyse it again, you can think of it as a compliment, isn't it?

Of course I didn't dare tell her that, because she would have smacked me then.

Now, let me take you back to the incident, the reason for the statement. One day, on our way to grocery, mother and I came across one of her friends, who on seeing me asked what was on my face?

'What was on my face?' I thought.

Has anyone ever looked at you and asked that?

Don't you think it is outrageously impolite?

'What's on your face?' Who asks someone that? Well, she was referring to the pimple on my face and I realised it.

This lady had no manners. Without any greeting or a smile, she popped that question on to my face. A question that was bigger and nastier than my pimple.

So, I gently replied that 'it is probably like the one that she gets on her ass'.

I don't recollect whether I said 'ass' or 'giant ass 'but she was dramatically taken aback by that reply and my mother was very furious about what happened, and she asked me to apologise immediately, to which I agreed instantly.

I said, "I am so sorry for the pimple on your ass."

That was it. It was like a little bomb blast or a bum blast statement, my mother caught my hand, almost piercing through my flesh and walked off with me, after apologising to the lady.

One thing my mother knew was not to ask me again to apologise. She was sure scared at the thought of how much more damage I could cause to the already awkward situation that I had created.

When I handed that money into her hands, there was so much love and acceptance in her eyes. She peered into my purse to see if I had given it all.

I had given it all, with just a few notes left.

I am never sad to give away my money. I was sad that I would not have any money to execute my escape plan.

This meant I needed to get the money. Well, there was no theatre work booked anytime soon, so I resorted to the other one.

The one in which I was slightly more skilled than theatre. It was my innate ability to talk to the spirit! To the souls that have departed from this world, the minds that are wandering the netherworlds, the ones who have exited to a different realm, the ones that are stuck in between. You get the point!

In short, there was always people who wanted to talk to the dead and they would reach out to me, and I helped them to communicate and in return they paid me cash.

My sister was aware of most of my doings. She knew that I met people and channelled the solus of their beloved ones. She was creeped out and had asked me several times not to do it, even though she said she did not believe in any of it.

If I remember it correctly, she used the word 'bullshit' to describe my work. She firmly believed that me talking to the souls were all just an imagination.

I don't know what the truth was, but when I called on the spirits, I spoke whatever the spirits would guide me to, it did bring some consolation to the living. Also, not everyone did such speciality jobs, it was a unique gift, but not so appreciated by the general community.

Alright, I might be speaking on behalf of the dead with an understanding what the living wanted to hear. But I still feel, I had a unique take on the whole thing.

One day, when I was small, I remember pointing at one of my father's uncle and saying that he was going to die.

My mother smiled awkwardly and said, "Now don't say like that alright? You got to respect your elders."

"I respect him, he's going to die tomorrow." I said again.

My mother was struggling to get me to shut up and not make such a big deal. But everyone's eyes spoke the obvious, 'what I said was not cool.'

It was even worse the next day when he died. My mother decided not to take me to the funeral and gave me the looks, like I was responsible for his death.

She herself, paid only a quick visit.

'You got to stop saying nasty things,' my parents and my sister advised. 'You got to think before you speak and be normal.'

Hence, I decided to take up theatre and I did a lot of acting on stage and the acting element just flowed into my other aspects of life as well. Like at home, in school, with friends, strangers and when calling the spirit. Everything needs a little drama, a little twist and some surprises.

After my money was put up for family benefits, I had to resort to other plans, so here I was in one of my friend's cousins place, who wanted to know why a certain person had committed suicide.

I went in and as per all the information that was given to me, I started my work. I called her name, "Nisha, Nisha, someone's here for you with questions. He wants to know why you killed yourself?"

I paused and called her name again, "Nisha". "Answer me Nishaaaa..." I said aloud dramatically. Then I stopped and afterwhile I said, she killed herself because she felt cheated.

There was 200 Rupees in my pocket at the end of that job.

I wouldn't say I was operating completely on a fraud level. Because I never intend to do it that way, I am truly interested in paranormal activities, and I do sometimes sense something extraordinary. Like a feeble cry, or someone calling out my name or a feeling that someone is near me, beside me. At times I even feel like someone touched me.

Again, who is going to listen to a 17-year old's crazy tales especially if she's going to speak about peculiar things.

"Mamma, have you ever felt Déjà vu?" One day I asked.

"What's that?" My mother asked.

"Like you have been in this moment before." I spoke.

"Everyday!" was her reply.

"You do feel?" I asked.

"Every day, I wake up at the same time, make breakfast, send you people away, get into cooking, cleaning. It's the same moment over and again.

Only I did not know it was called 'some kind of Woo.'" She told me.

I wasn't too shocked by that answer, I told her, "Mamma, you need a life outside of your housework. What you are feeling, or doing is not Déjà vu."

"Housework takes my whole day; what do you expect me to do? Drama? Dance? It's for you young girls. This is the life of a woman. This is reality." Saying she walked away.

Everyone has the capacity to take an extra step and perceive the world at a higher level.

Yet, we often choose to simply move through it, avoiding the view from above, passing through the middle until we reach the end—until death arrives.

What if we took that extra steps to expand ourselves, to see what's hidden and read the code?

"Read the code? First you try to solve your maths problems, then try to read the hidden code." My sister said teasingly.

"You cannot read my diary." I jumped at her.

"I can and I choose to." She replied holding onto my book which was titled 'SECRET DIARY.'

"You shouldn't be doing that. It's a crime. Punishable under law." I told her.

"That maybe in your world, where you live with codes." She said and started to laugh wildly.

I laughed too because I felt it was funny. I was fine with it because I had managed to keep my secret safe. My plan! All the blueprint was only in my head.

Because the blueprint was small and did not have many details on it.

I hadn't told anyone that I was slipping away that night. Breaking barriers to step out into the night all by myself to experience an extraordinary courage.

It was my own crafted and curious adventure. I wanted to slip away into the dark night, open my eyes and ears, sense the blackness it holds and feel the fear. I wanted to know if the fear was true, I wanted to know how cruel the night was and how deep was the unseen.

I wanted to know what was hiding in the dark, who was hiding in the dark? Would I survive or die this night?

So, I planned to go out by myself, travel till the movie theatre, watch a good movie, enjoy some great food and be back. I wanted to know if this was possible.

This must seem like a simple task but in our town, no girl of my age would step out at night, especially to watch a movie all by herself! No one goes to movies at night, except if you are a man with your gang of friends or if you are going out with your family which would include an adult male member.

Given the circumstances that I was in, being a girl and alone, I could ideally take help of someone to get around, but I chose not to do that for various reasons.

Firstly, I did not want them to bail out on me and secondly, what if they don't act according to the plan, then all of this would end in a big disaster.

So, keeping the above reasons in my mind, I thought to execute solo.

That's how I mostly work, mysterious, only depending on the most dependable person, which was - myself.

My house would be around 30 Kms away from the movie theatre.

If I step out, I do not know what can happen, or unfurl? Who are the people lurking around, what danger does it hide? I don't know, I can only imagine the worst.

I waited for everyone to settle down for the night. Dinner time went by with small talks. I had to be careful, because this was the time when everyone paid attention to one another.

This was the time when my father noticed his daughters and checked if everything was all right with us and enquired if school and studies were going well for us.

Any kind of clues or facial expression that would have raised a question had to be avoided.

Hence, calmness had to overcome the fear and anxiety that was building up. I tried to lay low and not to exhibit myself overly in front of everyone, to avoid attention and interaction and to just be there.

I helped clearing the dishes.

"Mamma, shall I put these in the fridge?" I asked softly while packing the remaining curry.

"You are helping a lot today," she said.

Was I? I thought, don't I do this every day? What does she mean by that statement?

"I am feeling sleepy, got to get up early tomorrow and study for the test." I said, justifying my kind nature that I had displayed earlier.

"Go and sleep, if you are feeling tired, Aarti and I will finish clearing up." Mum remarked.

"It's okay, I will help a bit," I said and quietly swept the floor, hoping that not another word would come out of their mouths.

"When is your next performance?" Mother appeared from nowhere with a question.

I was startled, but replied quickly, "Not got any at the moment."

Then in a teasing way she said, "what happened to you drama people, did you all get hit by real life?"

I laughed at that response with a very genuine like laughter. I did not want to engage in a back-and-forth conversation.

I had to keep things moving. Not too fast, just the right way and at the right pace.

"I think my stomach is upset." My father joined with his problem.

"Why???" I cried.

"I don't know my child." He said looking at me with a sad expression.

"Just gas maybe." Mother had an answer.

"Maybe some ginger will help." I said and wanted to close the matter fast.

"No, I will have jeera water" My father said.

"Okay," I said sadly

"You look upset?" My father looked at me and asked.

"No, it's just that you have too much gas all the time." I spoke.

*Jeera is cumin seeds.

23

"But it is of no use, we can't fill it in our gas cylinder," mother remarked laughing and then she switched on the stove to prepare jeera water.

I gladly helped with the jeera water,
cooling it to the right temperature
and giving it to my father quickly.

'You are so slow,' I almost said aloud.

"What's with you?" My mother nudged me.

"I have a test, and I need to sleep." I told her.

My mother was getting a bit furious now. "I told you to go and sleep."

My sister looked at me suspiciously.

After much waiting and cleaning and everyone finishing their toilet routine, the house was finally quiet.

My father had begun to snore, it was a lullaby for the family to slip into their slumber.

With everyone finally sleeping, the moment had arrived. All that waiting exhausted me.

I felt sleepy and very tempted to
chuck the plan. But I was a
disciplined and determined person.

I said to myself, 'I cannot do this
another day, this is it.'

When I snuck out from my home, that very instance, I was uncomfortable. I wanted to get back inside, be in my bed and not proceed at all with this nonsensical plan of mine.

So, why was I going for this?

Why was I not stopping despite everything in me wanted to stop and rush back?

Was I pulling myself into an unavoidable fate of mishap?

The fear was intense, exaggerated and my mind clouded.

I could not control it and my steps just kept moving further and further into that devouring night and all the feeling it encompassed.

That fear dipped a bit when I saw the light of a taxi. I soon waved to it, the car stopped, and I got in. Getting into that taxi was a moment of relief but I wasn't totally calm.

I was an open prey to anything unfortunate. The night was still alive, and I was in it.

The driver asked, "alone?"

"Two of us." I said casually. I could never stop myself from messing around with people. My friends often remarked that this habit could get me in real trouble one day.

"Two?" He replied in a surprised way which I had anticipated.

"What happened?" I asked him.

"Who two?" He replied.

I realised it was better not to distract someone when he was driving, that too at nighttime. Also, not to forget I was a passenger in the car.

"Brother, of course I am alone." I clarified. I am doing a project; it is part of my studies.

"What is part of your studies?" He asked again.

I wasn't sure how to answer that, so I told him that I was going to see a movie.

"Alone?" He asked again.

"Yes," I mumbled and turned my face to the window.

"Are you running away from home?" He asked glancing at me through the review mirror.

"No, I have to write a review for a movie, and I have to submit it tomorrow, so I am doing a last-minute work." I responded in a slightly agitated way.

The man went on, "I can tell you the review of any movie. I see all the movies."

"I will have to write a detailed one." I said.

He asked, "What kind of studies is this?"

"Movie making." I said softly. I hated telling lies.

"You are into films?" He asked cheerfully looking through the review mirror.

Saying 'Yes' I turned my face to the window again.

He understood it was a signal to be quiet.

When I reached the movie theatre, I knew I was going to be fine at least for some time, but I was so far away from home and my innocent family.

However, I was happy that I made it till there.

I got down from the taxi and thanked the man.

"Thank you for bringing us here." I said, unable to stop myself from executing a small prank on him.

"Us?" He said.

There it was that look I had hoped to get. A shock, a surprise, a little drama, a high moment.

I gave a weird smile and asked the invisible person to come with me and then I walked away. I stopped and turned around to wave at the Taxi driver who was still confused as to what was happening.

He sure had a story for the night, I thought. Even if I may or may not have one today.

Soon my eyes relaxed and began to observe some pleasant visuals. There were people talking and laughing with friends. There were more people than I expected. The night did not seem to bother them.

Sometimes you have a certain idea of something in your head but when you come face to face with it, you realise that it wasn't exactly like how you thought.

The fear of night began to disappear, night can also be friendly, I thought. It was like, all that I feared did not exist, it was just a compounded amount of fear that I had managed to create out of nothing as result of unknowing.

I was still uncomfortable. I think it was because at home, nobody knew I wasn't there. What if they found out?

I could not think of that. They would be so worried. Do I call them and let them know I am here?

My father could wake up to drink water and realise that I am not there. Maybe he may not. He never checks on us in the middle of the night, I thought. My sister could toss and turn or wake up at a sound, switch on the light and scream, discovering my disappearance.

Everyone would come running and wonder what happened to me. They would assume I was kidnaped.

As I was drifting away in my thoughts, my eyes caught onto something. I could not believe, it was the great actress **Kamala**. She was at the movie theatre.

31

I went towards her, she was alone. She greeted me with a warm smile. She was more than 60 years old, so radiant, so calm, and gracious.

She said she had come to see a movie.

I told her that it was a real surprise to see her and that I was thrilled to see such a popular star.

She asked about me and I told her my story, of how valiantly I stepped out to be here. She laughed and said that I was a stupid brave girl.

She asked, what made me do it despite being so scared.

"I don't want to be that scared. I want to break the fear that everything can go wrong if I step out at night. I wanted to break my fear that I will be hurt at night.

I no longer want to be scared to be alone at night.

I want to feel that I am independent, I can do it.

I don't want to feel trapped by the idea that being a girl will hold me back from reaching where I want to be."

"Sounds very interesting." Kamala said smilingly. "Let's get something to eat."

Was she really offering to eat together, with a simple girl like me? Do celebrities do that?

I shook my head in approval, but I am sure I looked enthusiastic and awkward at the same time.

"What would you like to have?" She asked politely.

"Anything is fine. I eat everything." I told her.

She told me to wait at the same spot till she got back with the food.

'She is such a sweet person.' I thought to myself. She has so much respect for another person. How do people get such good qualities?'

She bought a snack for both of us. We sat in a cozy corner and enjoyed that sumptuous meal of fried potatoes with special meat sauce, yoghurt, fried onions and celery.

"That was delicious," she exclaimed. I agreed with a big smile.

"So how do you feel now?" She enquired.

"I feel so much better but scared. In fact, worried about my family." I told her what I was feeling.

"Ah! now you, see? That feeling is going to be there till you get back safely. Maybe they know nothing, and they are all asleep or else they are heartbroken finding out you aren't there.

What do you say, do you want to go back or watch the movie?" She asked me.

I listened to her speak. I observed how young she looked, her gestures, her smile. Also, how meticulously she was studying me just like I was studying her. She was very gentle and non-judgemental.

"I have decided," I said. She looked at me, raising her eyebrows meaning, "What?"

Confidently I said, "I will watch the movie as I have come this far."

"Alright. Shall we watch together?" She asked.

"Sure!" I told her. I was thrilled at that question.

We sat together, watched a thoroughly enjoyable movie. I realised it was a good one because everyone around me was laughing.

I could at no point engage in it completely, but I assumed it was hilarious and was truly happy to know that people were enjoying. I was glad that I did choose a good movie to watch after all, even though I was not really into the movie.

How could I be? I was sitting next to the legendary actress Kamala; I wanted to pinch myself to truly realise the moment and not be lost in my anxious thoughts.

Besides the excitement of being at a movie theatre at an odd hour and meeting a film actress, I was worried thinking of home and the possibility of my family finding about my absence.

If I ever told anyone about what happened today, would they believe me? If I told them that 'I was with actress Kamala, watching a movie', they would think I 'm crazy. They would make funny remarks like 'Yes like the prime minister was in our house for dinner last night' and laugh it off.

But this was real. I was with her, we had food together, we talked, we enjoyed, and she cared for me.

It was out of kindness that she decided not to leave me alone and stayed with me so that I would be safe.

She was sitting next to me; I could feel her love and support. I know how magical she is on screen but how can someone be so charismatic in real life too.

She just met me, and I feel there is some kind of bond already. What is this bond we share? Who am I to her?

I felt that she was just not an actress that I have seen a thousand times on screen. Or was it enough to form an instant bond?

The familiarity of knowing her through screen, did it culminate to a connection for both of us? Can she feel so much love to anyone she sees because of the closeness and admiration that she sees for herself in their eyes?

After the movie, I clicked pictures with her. It was a digital camera and was a gift from my aunt from USA. I played back and showed her the pictures we clicked.

"Nice!" she said.

"I can send them to you." I replied.

"Oh, that would be great," she spoke. We exchanged numbers and then she put me in a taxi to go home. I saw her standing there waving at me, assuring me that it's all going to be okay.

I got back home and everything seemed fine. They were all sleeping unaware that I was away for such a long time.

I felt relieved being back home with a tiny bit of guilt lingering in my heart because of what I did. I would never want to try that again.

I slowly crept into my bed and slept peacefully. I felt a special kind of peace settling within me, that feeling which I was longing for all night. I was safe and everything felt like a dream and nothing more than that.

The next morning, I told my sister what I had done. It wasn't that I wanted to share it with her, but I felt it was better she knew that her sister could be dangerous at times.

I told her about Kamala too.

And her response was, "You are kidding. You don't even know how to tell a proper lie."

I asked her why I would tell a lie that would get me in trouble.

"I have no idea; you are unbelievable sometimes. So, you are telling me you had food with actress Kamala, the actress Kamala?" She asked me fiercely.

I knew she would not believe me. So, I took out my camera and then showed her my pictures with Kamala.

She looked at the pictures shockingly and shouted out "what the F?", then looked at me in a disturbed way. "You are so weird, with your weird unexplainable experiences... you crazy freak!" She shouted angrily.

I looked at her puzzled.

Why was she upset now? I had told her what I did.

Then she said, "You do know, right?"

I kept quiet. I felt something sinking in my stomach.

She spoke again, "actress Kamala passed away probably a month back?"

I stood there silently and thought to myself.

Yes, that was true. Didn't I know that? In fact, I remembered that I did know about her death. Somewhere in my head I knew that, isn't it? I am weird.

But that night I was with Kamala, and we were enjoying each other's company.

Why did I not freak out at when I saw her?

Why did I not feel that it was something odd?

Why was I okay with it?

Did I not perceive her as a dead person at that time?

I did probably. I know I did. But I just pushed that thought away and she became very alive in front of me.

She was there to support me. I knew that and she was aware too. Somehow, she sensed my fear, my loneliness and came by to help. She just stood by me, that kind soul, and I acknowledged her benevolence, her presence, and her power.

That is all.

My sister looked terrified. I did not know what the outcome of this was going to be. Would she tell our parents? Would I be treated like an outcast?

I did not say anything to her and could only hope she would be kind to me.

I can never explain what I felt or give a justifiable answer to why I behaved in that manner. Why a certain knowledge or truth made no relevance at that time of interaction.

You may not comprehend this, but one thing is certain, it's not about me being weird. It is not about me being a daredevil or unconventional.

It is about me able to see love when it is around.

The night holds a peculiar kind of vibe and mystery. The moment you step into darkness, the unseen becomes extraordinary.

This short story recounts a paranormal experience, and it's likely that many of you have had similar, unexplainable encounters that lingered in your thoughts for days, or perhaps even left a lasting impact.

This story is special in many ways. It is dedicated to the mysteries of the night—the enigmatic power that keeps something hidden. This story is for the ones who may never know what freedom at night is like, even when that adventurous spirit in you wants to dive into the most dangerous depths, you know you can't.

I also dedicate this story to the ones who have lost to the night.

This story acknowledges great minds who makes conscious choice to recognize the love around them. It may sound cliché, but it's true: love is all around us, and you must open all your senses to feel it. Once you do that, the world turns magical for you.

Keep your spirits high, **Rose Butterfly**

Short Story #2

PARALLEL

No one can deny the life that you lived!

One look at him, and you'd think, he's a good-looking guy. And with just one interaction, you'd know—he's a charmer.

It wasn't that he was trying; in fact, his appeal seemed almost effortless.

The way he carried himself, the attentive focus he gave each person who spoke to him, the kindness in his voice, the neatness of his appearance, his golden hair, and those eyes that seemed to twinkle with a life of their own—all of it added up in a way that naturally drew people in.

Dressed simply yet strikingly in a crisp white shirt and dark brown pants, he appeared relaxed and confident.

As he stepped up from his seat to address the large crowd in the packed auditorium, the crowd cheered and clapped and welcomed him. He had a perpetual smile on his face which gave a soft look, making him seem approachable and warm.

The audience leaned forward; each person ready to pose their questions to the scientist who had shaken the very foundations of his field.

Earlier that afternoon, he had sat down for an interview with Joan Haily from *The Face* magazine, discussing his timeless contributions to science.

As she watched him from across the table, she couldn't help but notice how unexpectedly youthful and attractive he was. It struck her how this man could be both a genius and a captivating figure—a combination that seemed almost too good to be true.

He welcomed her warmly, offering to get her something to drink. When she requested a coffee, he slipped into the kitchen and returned moments later with two steaming cups. She hadn't anticipated that he would be making the coffee himself.

"Don't you have someone to help around?" she asked, surprised.

"For making a coffee?" He laughed softly. "I think I can manage that."

There was something simple yet touching about it. Joan sipped her coffee, thinking this is a special one.

Taking out her recorder, she announced, "I'll be recording this, just to make things easier."

"Of course," he replied with a nod. "Go ahead."

She glanced at him with a wry smile. "You're aware that you're known as a heartthrob scientist, right?"

His lips quirked up slightly. "Heartthrob... scientist... they're just labels, aren't they? I try not to get too attached to names. I'm just following my heart, really."

"You make it sound so simple," she replied, a little amused. "But that's not how people see it. You're practically a sensation, bringing science to a whole new level."

"Science has always been there," he answered, still smiling. "I'm just lucky enough to be able to uncover something."

"Are you trying to be humble?"

"Are you trying to be cheeky?" he countered with a playful grin.

She laughed visibly. She was hoping for something more sensational, a crack in his charming exterior. But he remained as composed and polite as ever, that same endearing warmth never slipping.

"Any love interests?" she asked, trying to edge a little closer to something personal.

"Not that I know of," he replied, brushing it off with ease.

"Alright then," she leaned in, "tell us about some of your key findings."

"There's the idea that our universe might exist within a larger, parent universe," he explained, his eyes lighting up with excitement as he spoke.

"Imagine our universe as a single bubble in a cosmic foam, surrounded by other bubble universes.

Each one could have formed through a process called 'eternal inflation,' where different regions expand at varying rates.

When some areas stop expanding, they create isolated bubble universes, each potentially with its own unique physical laws and constants."

He paused, letting her digest it. "These bubble universes might exist within a larger, higher-dimensional space. You could think of it as a multiverse, with each universe a tiny pocket within this vast cosmic structure."

"That sounds... incredible," Joan murmured, awestruck.

He continued, "There's also the pursuit to decode the universe's arithmetic—a quest to discover the ultimate set of equations that might explain everything. It's a journey through mathematics, across scales and disciplines, in search of the fundamental laws that shape everything."

"And have you cracked the math?" she asked, leaning forward.

"Almost," he replied, his tone thoughtful.

"Will it really change anything for ordinary people?"

"It means a lot for humanity," he said, "It will redefine how we view everything and shape our future. And let's not forget, ordinary people are part of every story."

"But I am not part of your story?' She responded.

"So, you are the common people? Is it?" He asked raising his eyebrow.

Then smiled and continued, "If you think science doesn't touch you, why are you here doing this interview?"

"I meant," she clarified, "will it change anything in our everyday lives?"

He paused, then shrugged. "Hard to say just yet."

"How do you feel after all that hard work and finally being recognized as a success?" she asked.

"Life feels very different now," he admitted, a rare hint of vulnerability crossing his face. "It's like putting together the pieces of a puzzle and seeing the final picture.

There's a joy in that—what I feel now is about a thousand times more than that. I've been working non-stop, night and day, totally immersed. Right now, it feels good to just be here, relaxing a bit and enjoying this attention."

She smiled, satisfied with his answer, as the interview wound down. But his day wasn't over yet. He had a lecture that evening, followed by a party organized in his honour by The Fundamentals Club, which consisted of scientists and researchers of various scientific field.

That evening, dressed in his usual simple elegance, he moved easily through the party. At a glance he realised that they were mostly familiar faces. The event was lively, and he graciously acknowledged each person who approached him, answering their questions

---

But as his eyes scanned the room, they landed on an elderly man standing alone, watching him with a knowing look.

Something about the man seemed familiar, and curiosity piqued, he made his way over.

"Do we know each other?" he asked, sensing a strange familiarity.

"Not in this universe," the man replied with a smile.

"Is your family not here with you?" The man asked.

"Ah! no...no. They don't come with me to the parties and stuff." The scientist replied.

The man said with a smile. "We never see them. Where are you hiding them?"

"Am sorry, who are you?" He asked.

"A detective," the man said, his tone both casual and pointed. Simon"

Are you spying on me or something? He asked the man.

"Should I be?" Simon replied with a grin that suggested he knew more than he was letting on.

Meeting the man did not feel strange, but rather like a conspiracy, like someone was onto him.

After days filled with relentless interviews, crowds, and conversations, he finally felt the exhaustion settle in.

He welcomed the quiet of his home, free of the questions, the flashing lights, and the endless praise.

Taking a deep breath, he closed his eyes and submersed himself to a soul-full rest.

How many days did that sleep last, who would know?

With no family or close friends around him, there was nobody to check on him.

The scientific community would likely be content to let him disappear for a while, perhaps even a year if he needed it.

At a certain point of time, after his sleep, he sat up. He felt the warmth of the sun and its bright light hitting him.

On the wall in front of him was a large poster of a Singer named Simon Stellar. He looked at the picture, sensing a kind of familiarity. But there was something else, he also felt the warmth of her presence.

There she was. He observed how gently and easily she walked towards him.

"Here, your coffee", she said.

"Past few days have been tiresome for me" he said softly.

"Oh really," she remarked. "What did you do?"

"What do you mean? It was big and endless. The findings, the interviews. I am exhausted."

She looked at him blankly.

He thought, 'why is she looking at me like that, like she does not know anything, like what I am saying doesn't make any sense?'

"The last few month's I saw you almost every day, climbing the stairs up to the library, with a pile of books in your hands, sometimes I saw you at the bus stop.

I saw you sipping a coffee looking lost at something.

I remember we met at the community centre regarding the renovation of the park, and you smiled at me. Yes, I remember you feeding the birds in the city square.

I remember seeing you once in a while somewhere. Sometimes we waved, other times you don't see me," she chuckled.

"I came in today to just check on you because I felt that you don't even seem to notice me."

She spotted the distress on his face. She saw how worried he was about explaining it all.

They looked at each other, wondering what was happening?

Then, she sensed something which only she was capable of.

She realised that he was leading another life, something that only he knew of. Where? And how? She did not know but she was willing to trust him, and he realised that she was kind and open to believing him.

"No one can deny a life that you lived," she said in her mind and then aloud, and it travelled more than words, into his heart.

They saw that truth in each other's eyes.

He knew that what she said earlier about seeing him in different places were all true.

They both weren't lying. Because he did the impossible and she sensed that it was possible.

They smiled and that smile grew into laughter.

He was living more than one life.

And he was glad that she had absolutely no doubt about it.

"See you around" she said and started to walk away.

"You should know that there are people who cares for you." She looked at him again and spoke.

"You have always cared for me Julia; from the time I can remember." He said acknowledging everything that happened between them.

Then she left him and went to her appartement.

Getting back to her place, she was unable to rest. What she had was an unusual experience, most likely something that she may not be able to share with anyone.

But she had to put down this extraordinary experience. So, she wrote.

'I came across my friend today. Someone whom I knew from a very young age. Someone who studied with me, played with me and has always been kind to me. He is a remarkably wonderful person. So calm, very gentle and someone so warm to be around.

I have known him for so long now, he has not many friends. At least that's what I think. I do not know; I never see him with anyone.

I do visit him once in a while, because I feel an urge to just go and check on him.

But today I have been opened to a new world, his world.

It may be difficult to believe me, but I have sensed that truth.

"Today, I met not just my friend, but a man who led parallel lives."

No one can deny the experiences that you have had. Who are they to judge? They have not lived your life or felt what you have felt. There may not be many who can resonate with you, but somewhere, out somewhere in this world, there might be at least one who can.

It's just that, sometimes that person is very hard to find. Again, this world works in mystical ways, even though we say it works in an organised and systematic way.

In this half-proven reality that we exist in, anything can happen; the possibilities are endless. Remember, each one of us is only truly living our own story, our own perception, and that is all that is real to us.

What is your story? Remember to craft a good one.

Good Luck, **Rose Butterfly**

Short Story #3
MEANIE CAT!

I Love You!

Sigh!

If I were to ask you, if you've ever had those sleepless nights, when you felt tiredness overcoming every cell of your body, and yet it refused to surrender to the night.

And did those nights ever mean anything significant to you?

You would most likely tell me how common they are.

You might tell me that such nights are neither fascinating nor have been ever to be important but rather a too familiar occurrence, unwelcome like an annoying companion lingering stubbornly at your side, refusing to leave no matter what you offer.

Irritating and exhausting! That's what it is. Isn't it? All you would want is to fall asleep or for time to simply pass.

I would agree too, they are just torturous nights that eventually fade when you least expect, finally resigning, releasing you from its clutches into the unknown realms of sleep.

But somehow, for me that night did not turn out to be just an experience of a sleepless night. It was an encounter of my entire existence.

Unaccepting and painful, but eventually it led me to a journey of liberation.

Yet, at those moments of tossing and turning, the only feeling I could truly grasp was a sense of agitation and nothing profound. To relieve myself from that uneasy feeling, I began to gradually tread through the memory lane of happy and pleasant thoughts.

Obviously, thoughts don't stay on a singular lane, they tend to wander, taking a ride of its own, and I was polite, and I took that offer to creep through all of it, because at that point I was willing to take anything to fall asleep.

My house had a moderate size backyard with Kohuhu trees planted as fencing trees. When I bought the house, the trees were already planted, and I was told that they did not need much maintenance.

It was true, they thrived with absolutely nothing. Initially, I contemplated removing a few of them, but I soon discovered a beautiful reason to keep them. They were home to so many wonderful birds.

Magpies, common mynas, pigeons, house sparrows, and superb fairy-wrens, five different species of birds visited my backyard. Some of them appeared so delicate and tiny, I think they are probably the young ones.

That night, my anxiety grew, and I glanced at the nighttime monitor of my eight-year-old, struggling to discern whether she had fallen asleep or not.

It wouldn't be good if she were still awake this late, like me. Keeping that monitor helped us to communicate with each other, say goodnight over and over again and see her eyes twinkle just before she slept.

After a while, I realized she had indeed drifted off. Although she appeared perilously close to the edge of her bed, thankfully she never fell off ever. I knew this because otherwise she would cry and come to my room; that never happened.

Still, I decided to go to her room and check. She was sleeping close to the edge, but she seemed fine, so I refrained from adjusting her position. I went back to my room once again trying to sleep.

I observed how well my husband was sleeping that night while I lay in my bed, impatiently waiting for the slumber.

In the mornings, the backyard is quite a place to watch and enjoy.

When the magpies are present, none of the other birds are around. Initially, the Myna weren't friendly to other birds as well, then probably they all held a meeting and sorted it out. Soon, I could observe a kind of harmony that had settled in and all of them had found their place in the backyard, without really bothering one another.

Though the galah is a common bird here in South Australia, I have never seen any my backyard. They are usually found in large groups. Every time I see the galahs; I get the sense that these birds never get a good night's sleep. It seems like they were discussing something important the night before and never found a solution. They always looked grumpy.

My flock of bird families were a community of its own. They sang, chirped, and had lively conversations. I truly adored them, and I walked very cautiously not to scare them away. When I say walk cautiously, I never stepped into the backyard, obviously they would fly off. I had to take delicate steps inside the house because they are so good at tracking movements and sounds.

I began to wonder if the sleepless night could be a symptom of early menopause. I was forty-four, an active woman who had a full, tiring day. I should have been able to sleep through the night with ease, unless there was some underlying change happening in me. I lay like that engrossed in my thoughts for some time until I heard the sound. A screeching ferocious sound.

To me it sounded like someone was being killed, I thought someone was being attacked in the neighbouring house.

'It's better to lay quiet and not check the danger; stepping out could put me in a threatening situation!'

That was the thought I had when I heard the sound, but it wasn't my reflex at all. I had to get up from my bed and see what was happening.

Even before I got up, I recognized the source of the commotion; a cat, possibly engaged in a fight with another cat, a mouse, or some other creature. I wasn't sure because it was dark, and I couldn't see anything.

I switched on the outside lights and through my sliding glass door I tried to have a close look at what was happening. The backyard looked calm, with trees appearing thicker and wild in the night.

Despite the quietness, it gave off the vibe of a crime scene. I saw feathers flying around, soft feathers all around. The wind was blowing them away. The cat had clearly attacked one of the birds, perhaps catching it off guard while it slept.

I knew this cat; it was our neighbour's cat, and it often visited my yard.

It wasn't that he was hungry or hadn't gotten enough food. He was a well-fed cat. He was fondly called 'Midnight' by my daughter.

'Midnight' was dark like deep night, hefty feline, with a big full belly, a light blue collar, and a commanding appearance. He often roamed our backyard or explored the neighbourhood, casting a knowing gaze my way.

I knew he particularly liked visiting my house, yet it was a mystery why a well -fed cat would assault the birds.

I couldn't brush off the fact that he had eaten one of the birds, just because there was a predator instinct in him.

I tried to look with my eyes wide open to see where he was, as I could not spot him anywhere.

I stood there feeling desperate, sad, lost, and confused. Then as I looked up again, I saw the cat--- that black meanie cat.

The cat looked at me, its eyes locking with mine in a way that felt strangely familiar, as though it understood me. What I saw after that shook my core, my existence and my understanding of everything around me. The cat was changing its shape. Its form began to ripple, distorting its appearance.

Then, before my eyes, the fur faded, the whiskers disappeared, and the sleek, feline shape morphed. In seconds, it was no longer a cat—it had turned into my son. He was standing there with that genuine gentle appearance, the same deep, knowing eyes.

I froze, unable to comprehend what had happened. My mind was racing with thoughts. I was caught between disbelief and wonder.

I watched in astonishment as he shifted from being on all fours to standing upright.

The following action that I took on seeing all of this was not a justifiable one to myself or my son. It was an impulsive one, one that lacked love and compassion.

I locked the door towards the backyard and that did not make me feel good. It broke my heart.

Did he kill that bird?

He stared at me with desperation, silently pleading for me to open that glass door and let him in.

But I did not nudge. I felt bad that I could not open that door. How could I turn so blind to my son? Poor thing stood there crying; crying like a baby, asking me to open and let him in.

I felt I could see feathers in his mouth, and I could smell a stink. My heart had grown hard, unable to hold on to the compassion that I was feeling deep within.

Am I this inconsiderate, unmerciful, and unkind to my own child?

How cruel am I?

The whole idea of my son sneaking around and turning into a cat was not something that I could digest but also there was another side to it. Why was he doing that?

Why did he have to take the birth of being a child and a cat at the same time?

The life of going through all of this pain, a dual personality. Why did he choose to carry the guilt of having to kill?

As I began to think, I felt sorry for my son. His sweet little face was looking at me for forgiveness. But I also felt sad for the bird, and I was angry at my son for not being able to stop being a cat and having a control of himself. For not resisting his instinct to be wild and choosing to kill that innocent bird.

I wasn't sure what I was feeling, was it anger or helplessness?

I couldn't bring myself to open the door, and my son began pounding on it, pleading to be let inside. Fear gripped me at some level. Just then, my daughter walked into the room and allowed him in, shouting something at me in the process.

He looked at me crying and walked away towards his room. I did not follow him. I quietly went to my room and lay down, being aware that I wasn't the sole decision-maker in this household.

The next day, my son tried to speak to me about what he was feeling. He wanted to share what he was going through. But I denied listening to him. Instead, I chose to watch him silently unable to accept whatever he was, piercing through his soul asking him-

'Why did you have to kill that bird? Why do you have to step out into the backyard at night? You don't need to do this.'

He met my gaze, then piercing through my soul replied, "Do you think I really have a choice?"

Perhaps he truly had no control over his actions. Maybe his transformation into a cat and the ensuing predatory behaviour were beyond his command. I don't know how, but I wanted to save him, I wanted to save my boy from the burden of being the 'bad cat.'

Time must have passed by. Not just days, may be years. But to me, it seemed like the next day. I had arrived at a new day like from a previous moment to the next moment.

This time, we were all gathered outside, witnessing a selection process unfold—a division and segregation of sorts. It did not look like a pleasant task but a fearful one, like being under the control of a leader.

This process determined who would undertake specific tasks, who would be moulded in certain ways, and who would undergo particular experiences, like the one my boy had.

The thought of that pained me. My dear child, will always remain as a 'cat boy' if that's what is assigned to him.

I wanted to scream, 'please stop, can he have a choice?' We stood shoulder to shoulder, waiting for our fate to be decided. Time seemed irrelevant, and I couldn't discern its passage.

I was locked in a perpetual cycle of existence. One thing I knew was that time was only meant for the decisions to take place. The order to go. I stood there for a while. Waiting.

This is me and my name is……

Oh! I am unable to recollect my name. But what I can remember about myself is that I am the mother. I have always been the mother. The great, talented, beautiful mother; the lady with all the good virtues. The kind woman. I am her and I am that. It's my identity, my assigned role.

Anybody who has ever dealt with me would say, what a pleasant person I am, they would say the nicest things about me. I am given some great qualities- trustworthy, hardworking, determined.

Also, I live with my family.

But today, I am here. I do not know if I have been here before, but I feel like I have undergone the same before, like I am going through a vicious loop. I stood there to continue my journey or may be to take on a new one. I wouldn't know. It was all the same. I had no choice, none of us had a choice. We were slaves.

Then, as the decision-makers prepared to deliver their edicts, a brilliant light filled my mind.

Something drew me in, and amidst the multitude of individuals awaiting their commands, I fell to my knees. My hands touched the ground, and I found myself on all fours.

The God was near me, I looked up, my head raised up slightly, and I spoke to God.

"This time let me be the cat. The well-fed bad meanie cat."

I had a glimpse of the Lord's face, a tiny glance. I think he was smiling. I do not know if the Gods have accepted my request, but I sure tried with my whole self. I did not see the expression on my son's, daughter's, or my husband's faces. They were standing next to me, but still, I did not look at them, how could I?

I was on the ground; I do not know what they felt or what they thought. But I was feeling good. I could sense the overwhelmed heart of my son pounding in gratitude.

I said in my mind. 'I want no gratitude; I want you to enjoy, being just a boy. Be just a boy my son, be free.

And I know, you will treat the meanie
cat, better than I ever would.'

I relinquished my role as the nurturing mother, the kind woman with an excess of virtues, to embrace a different existence.

"Did you? I heard someone say. A very clear distinctive voice spoke into my ears. Or did you live up to your true nature?" The voice asked me.

I shook in confusion and asked, "Who said that?" **Meow!!!**

This is my favourite work in this collection, as I navigate through minds, trying to understand various roles and struggles. When this story emerged, I knew I had to put it down, even though stepping into the shoes of both mother and son was intensely painful.

This story is dedicated to those tormented souls trying to find peace amidst the overwhelming task of rescuing their loved ones who are trapped in unimaginable circumstances, problems and illnesses that they cannot explain to anybody. Your dear ones, they remain as the unwelcome beings of society.

What more could you ever do to save your children, Mamma?

You are so powerless, struggling between what's right and your love. Hope you are empowered with immense strength, wisdom, patience and most importantly a good support system to get you through and guide you.

Sincerely, Rose Butterfly

Short Story #4

CONVERSATIONS WITH YOU

Bye-Bye Miss American Pie.

I moved in pain. Unsure and broken, in anxiety and in uncertainty. All of what was happening was scary. I was waking up from death.

I was struggling to get up and grasp the world around me. I was waking up and I knew it wasn't just another day; I felt the heaviness of that struggle and nothing around me made sense.

I tried to hold on and do my best, but I did not have a clue of what was happening. I did not understand where I was or who was around me.

"Where am I?"

Finally, with much difficulty I said those words aloud or maybe it was just a mumble that no one heard.

I felt like I was taking a lumbering step into a new space. I was moving myself from an existing life to a new one. What was I doing?

In that moment of chaos, I could not comprehend what was happening nor what going to unfold. How could I? After all, that day was just the beginning of a new understanding. I was waking up from a tedious and what seemed like an endless state of coma.

I was struggling and weeping while stepping into the current reality. All of this would give anybody a fair idea of my situation and my state of disorientation, anxiety and agitation.

Anyone watching me would understand that 'the waking up' was not an easy moment. However miraculous it may seem; it was like being born again.

It is no doubt that this whole event is one of a kind and it is a blessing to get back your life. But for me it was like hitting a wall of a new reality.

I do agree that there is nothing more precious than your own life and the joy of spending it with your loved ones. What could be more joyful for someone like me than being reunited with the family. I was getting back all that I lost.

And thus, there ends my story. Ideally, my story should have ended there. I was in coma, and I am fine now. A perfect end.

But for me, it was like a crack opening up beneath me as I took every step forward hence after that.

For many around me, this is the end of my story. Beautiful! Miraculous and sentimental! For the news channels, for magazines and for podcasts, my story ends with this and a big warm smile. This is all the bit I share, the miracle of being back and living again.

Something tells me, this is where I should stop sharing and say no more because if I truly take you through my journey, you will begin to suspect my sanity and say that 'it is all in my head.'

And I would hate that. I would not like you being judgemental about my experiences and my reality. So, maybe I should stop myself from sharing anything further and end this wonderful story right here.

But... what if you are someone out there who is like me and is looking for an answer, eager to hear about exceptional experiences, something that tells you that you are not alone in your own unique tale. Or maybe you are someone who believes in the craziest possibilities. If then, I am obliged to share my bit. Because one's story is never truly one's own.

We all live entwined in a complicated and yet in a simple way.

For those of you who wants to continue with your day not wanting to know anything beyond the normal that you see, you need to stop reading right now.

*Because my story is a unique one, an
exceptionally remarkable one and it
is only for those who are willing to
open their mind a bit wider. Who
are willing to acknowledge that
perceiving something extraordinary
is part of life and there is nothing
eerie about it.*

That day when I was waking up in the hospital, I was disoriented and weak, I had not much awareness of the current situation or what had happened in the past.

I was struggling in mind and in my body.

During that time a lot of moments flashed in my mind. It was varied and undefined clutter of thoughts and I felt it was piercing through me to tell me something.

I was struggling to recall where I was or what was happening to me.

Then I decided to take it all in a calm manner, so I looked closely at myself and was shocked to see me.

A self that was not me.

This is the best possible way I can describe the scenario. An understanding that what you see is not you. Then what is the truth?

But I stayed calm enough to not shout or perhaps I was lost enough to be silent.

Not recognising myself I stood there for a while but then I soon realised I wasn't standing at all.

I was lying down in a bed, in a hospital. Soon there was a rush of everything. The world around me became a blur of people, hurried footsteps, and incomprehensible conversations.

Amidst everything and anything,
there was only one thing I searched
for—my family.

Not the people who were surrounding me at that time, but the ones I had been driving to see, desperately trying to reach home before the accident.

Where were they? Why did they not come?

Were they not informed about me?

These questions raced through my mind, but I felt strange to ask them to the old lady who was crying next to me, even though she was my mother.

Was it strange that I couldn't ask her where my wife and kids were?

The doctors attended to me and after a while I was asked to get some rest. So, when I got a chance I asked the nurse, "do you know where my family is?"

"Your mother is outside, don't worry." She said in an assuring tone.

"Is there anyone else?" I asked her again.

"Oh! Your father is here too I think." she said smilingly.

Awakening from a coma is considered a miracle, but as I regained consciousness, I realized that I must have kept something incredibly important from my parents before the incident. Something like 'I have a wife and two kids.'

Nobody is telling me anything about them and that made me uncomfortable.

What I did not understand was why was this a secret?

I thought that I would continue to remain silent about it and find out why I hid the truth from them. There must be some reason.

Most obvious being they disapproved of her and hence I had a secret married life.

I could not stop thinking about them, especially my children and the journey they must have had to take without me, all of this made my heart ache.

Although I was grateful to have survived, despite three years having passed, I couldn't help but feel the weight of the missing moments. I thought about my little boy, Jeremy. He would be four years old now.

Would he recognise me?

It was important that I was part of what was happening.

The Now.

I was part of a medical miracle. A survivor. An answered prayer. I was part of many things and the one I was about to discover.

There was a lot of excitement, conversations, greetings, remarks, smiles, and joy around the scene of my departure to home. Fair enough, I thought! Afterall, it is a family reunion. One of a kind! Privileged to have experienced a miracle.

The journey home was not exciting for me for various reasons. Firstly, I wasn't comfortable getting into a car and travelling after my accident and then I knew I wasn't going to meet the people I have been missing so much.

How did I know? I always had an inexplicable sense of that truth, and it lingered with me all along.

I stared out through the window, watching the familiar landscapes pass by, yet everything felt foreign. My parents were silent, their expressions a mix of concern and hope.

I could sense the tension in the car, a unmistakable reminder of the life that I had left behind and the unknown future ahead.

When we arrived at our house, I noticed the surroundings, the quietness of the place and the view of a picturesque, lush mountains in the distance. There were trees meticulously planted along the footpath, and it moved vigorously in the wind, acknowledging my presence.

I felt a rush of nostalgia mixed with a strange sense of disconnection.

As I entered, I glanced at the mirror that was in the hallway, there was something undeniably different about me.

I peered closely at me, and a shiver ran down my spine. It was a reality I didn't want to face, but at the same time, I couldn't tear myself away from its grasp.

The mirror revealed a face that resembled mine. But I could not look at that image for a long time because my eyes pulled me to a time where I was with 'them,' my darlings.

My children, their laughter, the playing, their curly hair. I wanted to meet them.

"Come on in," my mother said and gently held on to my hand and walked me in.

---

*The walls were adorned with photos
of my childhood, family vacations,
and school events, and some of them
sparked something in me.*

Every corner of the house made me realise, I had lived in that place and have been in those room so many times. The windows, the furniture; they all looked familiar, homely and yet I was sensing something uncomfortable.

My family had just a small circle of friends; no one had come to greet us, just a few phone calls enquiring about me.

My parents, their quiet, orderly, and timid disposition made me feel that they were distant from their true selves in so many ways.

I could clearly see the heaviness of their life on their faces, a tale of migration, of finding a place to call home, overcoming differences, and forging new relationships.

But above all, in their face, I saw a smile of relief, an answered prayer and a glimpse of my face. They were so happy to have me back.

"Welcome home" my mother said softly, with opened arms, her voice slightly trembling as she said my name.

"Thanks, Mum," I replied, forcing a smile. "It feels good to be back."

I ventured into the rooms, each step filled with an uneasiness and a longing for someone.

The clothes in the closet, the scent of perfume lingering in the air—I could recollect it now, but I realised that there was a part of me that never felt belonged.

I did not belong to this house, to the family that I was with. Disconnection was the most familiar feeling I felt, even after all these years.

It was not their fault; they had passed on to me something inherently and unknowingly. I carried a

trace of disconnection every now and then. A feeling that I took on from my parents through their stories, their discussions and their journey which I was obviously a part of.

But love had dispersed all of that for me for a while and I wanted to feel that again.

It wouldn't be right to deny but I was aware of the life that I lived, and it was not here.

The next few days were a blur of doctor's appointments and rest. My parents were kind and attentive, but I could see the worry that was etched into their faces.

They tried to keep things normal, but the elephant in the room was impossible to ignore. Would I ever be completely okay?

Determined to piece together my past, I began exploring the house. In the attic, I found old photo albums, yearbooks, and boxes filled with mementos.

I spent hours sifting through them, hoping to trigger some memory, some connection to the person I used to be.

One evening, I stumbled upon an old diary tucked away in a drawer. I read those entries, probably made in those teenage years about some crushes and my dreams and that was it.

There was no clue or anything that I could attach to my mystery life. Honestly, I felt disappointed like everything was slipping away.

What was my love life like?

Should I inquire about it to my parents? Seated at the dinner table, surrounded by a lavish array of food, I observed the spread that my parents had prepared.

The doctors had advised them to take things slowly, not to overwhelm me with too much information or people at once.

So, they just showed love in ways they could. And food was definitely at the top of the list.

I could hear the rumbling in my stomach, so I decided to eat before delving into conversation. My plate was filled up with succulent chicken legs, crispy potatoes, vibrant vegetables, tender prawns, delectable cutlets, colourful fried rice, and even nachos and popcorn. As I savoured the flavours, I mustered the courage to bring up the subject.

"So, did I have a family?" I asked, my voice in an unusual pitch with anticipation.

"No darling, you have been single for a while," replied mum.

"You mean the three years, while I was in coma?" I smiled.

They looked at each other and laughed gently.

"Yeah that, and even before that," she continued.

That revelation left me astounded. "So, I don't have a family?" I inquired, desperately hoping for a different answer.

"Well, you could have one now," mum gently hinted.

This is just unbelievable!

They saw the disappointment on my face and mum said. "Why don't you catch up with some of your old friends."

"Like whom?" I asked

"Of course, you may not remember much, but do you remember Emily?"

"Which Emily?" my father asked as he was taking another serve of fried rice.

"You forget everything too fast," mum got a bit annoyed with my father. "Don't you remember Emily now?"

I wasn't sure how to respond to the whole thing.

"I know Emily." I raised my hand and said, and they looked at me worried.

"I'm so glad to hear from you," Emily exclaimed when I called her.

"I need your help. Can we meet up?" I asked, trying to keep my voice steady.

"Of course. How about the old café we used to go to?"

"Sounds perfect."

The next day, I met Emily at the café. She looked just as I remembered— warm, friendly, and a smile that grew dimples on her cheeks.

"I've missed you so much," she said, hugging me tightly.

"I am sure I must have missed you too," I said; to which she responded with another hug.

"So, what did I miss?" I asked her.

Over coffee, Emily filled me in on the past few years. She told me about her life, her job, and the mutual friends we had lost touch with.

"And what about Tom?" I asked casually.

"Which Tom?" She looked surprised.

"Which Tom do you think I am asking about?"

"I don't know. Which Tom are you asking about?"

"Maybe I am confusing it with someone else?" I quickly said.

"Is it? She leaned forward in a concerned way. You may be then asking about Jay? The guy I used to date?"

"Not him." I said.

Emily tried to help. "Is it Pete? The guy you met at the library and became friends with."

"No...no.... it's okay. Do you know anyone by the name Raziya?" I asked her and immediately felt like I probably should not have asked her that.

Emily looked lost again as she responded, "Who is that now?"

"I guess you don't know then." I said looking at her blank face.

"What are you saying?" Emily held my hand.

"It's alright, maybe I am a bit overwhelmed with all the information and pictures." I had to say something to get out of the awkward situation.

"Hmmm...mmm. You got to take things slow. Understand? Your folks are so anxious about you." She reminded and I nodded in agreement.

Driven by my desperate urge to find answers to what was happening, I decided to visit my old school.

I didn't have a clear plan, but I thought to just go ahead and be there and let things follow. Perhaps seeing children and the environment would help me connect with the memories of my son Jeremy.

I arrived at the school just as the children were being let out for recess. The sound of laughter and the sight of children running around brought a bittersweet smile to my face.

I wandered through the playground, watching the kids play, hoping to spot someone who might trigger a memory.

"Can I help you?" a voice asked from behind me.

I turned to see a woman in her early fifties, with kind eyes and a warm smile. "I'm sorry, I was just... visiting. I used to go to school here," I explained.

"Ah, a former student! I'm Mrs. Turner, one of the teachers here. What's your name?"

I told her about the accident and what had happened as a result of that. "I am trying to reconnect to my past. So, I was hoping to find something familiar here."

"Why don't you come inside? Maybe a little looking around will help." She suggested.

Inside the school, I walked the hallways, peering into classrooms. Mrs. Turner pointed out old photos on the walls, class pictures where I saw a younger version of myself. It was like stepping into a time capsule.

We entered the library, and I felt a rush of nostalgia. The smell of books, the quiet atmosphere—it was all so familiar.

I walked to the back of the room, where a bulletin board displayed class projects. One of them caught my eye—a family tree project.

"Mrs. Turner, do you know if the school keeps records of old projects?" I asked, feeling a surge of hope.

"We do have some. They're archived in the basement. Would you like to see?"

"Yes, please."

In the basement, Mrs. Turner and I sifted through boxes of old projects. Then I saw a folder with my name. It was adorable. There were so many pictures and writing. As I was sifting through it, something caught my eye. It was a drawing that I did.

The picture had me, my mother, my father and a boy. Next to the boy's drawing, it was written 'This is Jeremy.'

"Who added this boy in my family picture?" I asked, my heart pounding.

Mrs. Turner looked puzzled. "I'm not sure. It looks like it was drawn by you. Is it a sibling?"

I shook my head to say no.

"Then maybe a friend." She said looking at me puzzled. "Who knows maybe someone from the class." She added.

I felt it rather shocking to see the name Jeremy added into a drawing that was done so long back. It was probably drawn like 20 years ago.

As I lay in bed that night, I felt it was important that I came face to face with reality. I was unable to contain the truth. I needed to be where I needed to be.

Next day, I boarded a bus to Campbelltown. I walked down Agustus Street and made my way to the third house.

I went to the front door and rang the doorbell. As expected, nobody was home when I had arrived. Patiently, I waited until evening, across the street on the bench.

My anticipation was growing with every passing moment. And then, finally, they returned—my wife and my children.

They were real, alive, and looked happy. She parked the car, the kids got out and they went in. She looked at me and turned her face away and walked in.

I thought she had seen me, but she made no attempt to give me a second look. Why? Did she not recognise me?

I couldn't think much, my heart was feeling heavy. I tried not to dwell too much on my emotions but to keep moving. I knocked on the door.

My wife opened it, curiosity etched on her face. "Yes?" she inquired.

Unable to articulate anything much, I simply said, "Raziya, it's me."

She looked at me confused.

I quickly began to speak. "After the accident, I was in a coma for three years. I'm so glad, you and the kids are fine. I know the accident must have been tough on you and kids. I've missed you all so much."

She stood there, seemingly shocked. She abruptly called out, "Adam, please take care of Jeremy. I'm just stepping out and will be back in a bit."

Adam, my boy, came running, asking, "Where are you going, Mum?" His eyes fell upon me, and he gazed at me in a bewildered manner.

"Just talking with this lady here, that's all." Raziya replied.

Ignoring his scrutinizing look, I mustered a smile at Adam.

Confusion clouded his young face and a strained attempt to smile back eventually faltered, as if he made a conscious decision to withhold it.

The innocence he once possessed, had now given way to maturity. Then, summoning all my strength, I spoke to her, all the while deeply aware that she had not recognized the person standing before her—a harsh reality that had threatened to shatter any hope that was building up within me, rendering this heartfelt reunion to nothing more than a futile echo of my own longing.

"I know you don't recognize me, but I am Tom."

"What now? Alright, please step back. I am going inside." She sounded firm and cautious.

She should be, it is the craziest thing anybody would say. But I had to keep calm.

"Please listen Raziya." I pleaded with her.

"How do you know my name?" She asked.

I said, "Exactly, think about it, how do I know your name. Don't you want to know?"

She stood there looking at me. So, I continued to speak, hoping she would listen.

"I was driving that day, trying to reach home. I was listening to the radio, and I had switched the station and heard a song. What happened after that was very fast. I remember a car hit mine. I remember the accident. I know that my life stopped for three years, and my parents were grief struck by what had happened.

What I don't understand is the person I am now.

Am I crazy or am I dreaming? What is happening?"

She was quiet again. She looked shocked and indifferent seeing me.

She was trying hard to find words, to say something to me. But both of us did not know how to deal with the intensity of that moment.

Then, Raziya broke the silence, gesturing for me to come inside. And so, I entered inside our beautiful home—the place that meant everything to me.

I saw Jeremy, my little boy. He had grown tall, just like I had imagined.

"When did the accident happen?"

In a clear voice I said. "25th February 2016."

"Hmmm...." She let out a heavy sigh.

As emotions flooded through me, the doorbell rang, waking me from my thoughts. Raziya hurried to answer it, her actions betraying the presence of someone else in her life.

And though it shattered my heart, I knew that life moved forward, and I had to accept it. I had to be mature, act cool, and embrace the reality before me.

A gentleman entered, wearing a light blue shirt and brown pants. He was around 6 ft tall, well-built and attractive. Seeing him, my breath caught in my throat.

"What? That's Tom. That's me," I said quietly.

I had to face the reality of what I was aware of. I had to deal with it. And to be honest, is it not why I was there?

My parents never discussed the disconnection that we felt at times in our life. It was as if that's how it was meant to be.

New place, few friends, sometimes too alone on occasions, holidays and festivals. That was what our days were most times. It was not like we chose a quiet life but that was what we got as part of moving to an unfamiliar territory.

Three lonely people in a house. I would often tell my parents to fix playdates for me or have sleepovers, but they would just avoid the topic. I never had a sleepover until I was 18 years old. All that silence and pretending to be unaffected by everything that was happening around me, made me feel incomplete.

It made me feel like I wasn't spreading my wings. I was living a confused life.

Now this connection, what I felt was real and yet so mysterious.

"Well, who do we have here?" said the man.

In a casual way Raziya introduced us.

"Tom, meet Tom."

That introduction was unexpected. But it was also enough to get us to sit down and discuss what the hell was happening?

It was more evident on Tom's face who was absolutely perplexed to find me, a lady by the name of Tom.

Honestly, I was glad that they were willing to sit down and listen to me. At that time, I did not think much about their side of the story. I always thought, it was all about me having an unusual experience. Not for once did I think that they would connect to it.

We sat down and I shared my experiences with Tom and Raziya.

---

*I told them about my years in coma
during which I lived a life
experiencing being Tom, living with
Raziya and Kids in this house.*

I told them that, when I was waking up from coma, I wasn't waking up as me but as Tom and seeing myself in a woman's body was a shock.

"At the same time, it was not like I did not exist in me. Within moments of waking up, I felt connected to myself, but I could not let go off my memories, the feeling of love and my children. That was all very real.

I tried my best to take every day as being me, but I still had the yearning to be here. I wanted to think all of this as just a dream but then I thought what if it is real. What if you people actually existed."

They did not look at me in disbelief. They looked at me and heard everything that I said in complete acceptance.

---

*A profound level of understanding
and trust arose in us.*

In that moment, I felt an immense gratitude, a deep appreciation for their willingness to listen and empathize with the tumultuous journey that I had gone through.

"The accident happened 25th February 2016," Raziya added.

"Oh! You see..." Tom spoke.

"Yes," I responded. I wasn't sure what was happening. But Raziya motioned with her face asking Tom to go ahead and continue speaking whatever he was intending to share, which made me realise there was something more to the story.

"What happened?" I asked curiously.

"On 25th February 2016, I met with an accident as well. It wasn't as bad as yours. But I did have several injuries, and it took me a while to get back. I am still going through treatment."

As Tom was sharing, I felt like I was being pulled into someone's life, my mind raced with questions, 'who are these people? Why am I tied to them?'

I do not know if he could see the emotions on my face, but he continued to speak. "After the accident, it wasn't the same for me too. I would often tell Raziya that I felt the presence of another person, like I am having a journey together with someone whom I could not see but just feel.

It wasn't easy to articulate what I was experiencing but it all seems clear now. And I must thank you for this conversation." Tom looked relieved as he spoke.

We believed what I was having was a shared memory experience with Tom. He had met with an accident, the same day I had.

He survived the accident with minor injuries while I slept and experienced a life of love and family, with his memories woven into my consciousness.

Even when I understand all of this was a sharing of memories and experiences and the mastery of my brain to weave it all together for me to live a true life and that it did not actually or physically take place, I have to admit that I lived those three years or some of it or moments of it in an extraordinarily beautiful way and I am thankful to whatever phenomenon that made it happen.

It was all worth it.

We talked a bit more about it, this time a little more relaxed, like three people who solved a unique mystery, that only we could understand.

That understanding created a special kind of bond. An unknown, unexplainable, nameless bond.

Returning to the present, I had to confront the truth of who I was now—or perhaps, who I had always been, the person named Natasha. When did I stop being her?

Oh! it all seems so crazy now. I feel like I have stepped out of a dream.

I could feel my hair brushing against my face, my hands were cold, so I quickly buried them into the comforting pockets of my jumper.

I could sense the delicate golden chain on my wrist, and I was wearing my favourite blue jeans and a plain white top.

It was all me, the part of me that never was there and the part of me that was always around. The person that once felt lonely and the person that once loved.

I felt quiet inside. Then, an unthreatening surge filled my being, and I felt closer to me.

Before bidding farewell, I turned to Tom, pondering at the mysterious connection between us. "I wonder what brought us together," I mused aloud.

"Maybe it was that song on the radio...," Tom suggested, a flicker of recognition in his eyes.

"What was it again?" he asked, seeking confirmation.

"Bye, Bye, Miss American Pie, Drove my Chevy to the levee... I recalled, the lyrics resonating within me.

"Yes, that one!" Tom replied and joined in with a feeble hum.

"This'll be the day that I die.

This will be the day that I die."

His voice filled with a mix of wonderment and a knowing that only enveloped us.

In that moment, we realized the significance of that shared experience, a connection that forged through a song and an accident that altered the course of our lives forever.

As I walked away, accepting my new reality, I couldn't help but feel that those three years, whether true or imagined, were worth every ounce of drama, feeling, and life.

It was like a dream, but who is to say what reality is.

In this paradoxical existence, where I lived and yet not truly lived, I discovered that there was an unparallel, intricate and unseen thread of connection that held us all together.

I could see that thread was all around, connecting each one of us in more than one way. It was only when sometimes I chose not to see, I felt so lonely.

Without whatever that had happened to me, I wonder if I would have ever sensed something like this?

Would have I ever been able to love without barriers? I don't think so. I probably would have remained a judgemental fool.

This experience has opened my heart to unimaginable ways of connections that we share and a newfound perception of the power of love that I never would have envisioned possible.

I stepped out, not looking back, hummed an old song and walked away.

20 years ago...

A little girl draws a picture of her with her mother, father and a small boy.

In the drawing, they are all standing in a large green meadow, looking cheerful and relaxing. She had drawn a big smile on their faces.

There was a tall tree next to them and all around was yellow flowers.

"Who is that, the boy?" The mother asked the little girl.

"It's Jeremy." She said fondly.

"Who is Jeremy darling?" The mother asked curiously. "I don't know," the little girl replied wide eyed and innocent.

"The picture is beautiful." The mother said with a smile.

"Thanks Mum. I am going to take it to school and put it in my folder." Saying that, off she went into her room.

"Cute!" Mum said softly.

We all have a story, a journey that is unexplainable to others. What we see, how we perceive, the magic, the truth, the reality, are all our own little absurdities.

Sometimes, we may think that there is no one out there who may truly understand us and yet sometimes we meet people who instantly connects.

We are all different and one at the same time. That invisible thread that binds us is stronger and more magical than we can imagine.

This story is dedicated to all of you, who may sometimes feel that your story is a lonely one. No matter how twisted you may feel your life or situation is, there is always someone out there who is willing to listen, someone to lend you a helping hand, someone sent to take care of you.

Love, Rose Butterfly

Short story #5
ENTRAPPED

Who is with me?

If you look closely at the park bench, you'll see her.

She may seem like a figure who could almost blend into her background, like something that merges and dissolves into a vast canvas.

She may be sitting right there and yet you can sense that 'disconnection aura' that surrounds her. She almost seems like a mysterious person operating from another realm.

Is she now?

As the wind blows recklessly, her golden hair strands wildly sweep across her face.

Not disturbed by any of it, she calmly brushes her hair away, her eyes fixed onto something.

The bench beneath her is rich brown, polished and well-kept as compared to her faded jacket, which had seen years of wear.

She is wearing a turquoise dress that flows down to her ankles, giving her a look that's part wanderer, part watcher.

Around one ankle, she wears a silver anklet that catches the light, and just above it, a tattoo that may have a story to tell.

What's interesting about this young lady, at this particular moment is that she's in the 'gaze zone.' She is looking at something so intensely without being distracted by anything around her.

But what is she looking at?

Her eyes are locked on a single tree standing before her. A huge tree with a fat trunk, cracked and split, bleeding a sap that gives it a crystal-like shine in the sunlight.

But it's not the tree's decay that holds her focus.

It's the face.

A face that is hidden just beneath the layers of a particular spot on the trunk. To an untrained eye, it might look like a trick of the lines and knots, but she sees it clearly.

The face.

That face has giant eyes, a big nose and a wide mouth. The faces that she observes are never particularly expressive. Trina knows that beings like this don't want to be seen; they prefer to hide in plain sight, blurring into the edges of the world.

They are watchers, creatures from beyond ordinary perception, who slip into the ordinary landscapes of life—trees, rocks, structures—just waiting, hidden and doing whatever they are meant to do.

But she sees them. She always has. She has learned to pierce their disguises, to lock her gaze on them until they realize they cannot hide from her.

She knows they feel it too, the weight of her attention pressing into their guise until the façade slips, and the faintest trace of unease flickers in their gaze. It's why they don't move or react; remaining still, silent, is their only defence.

Trina has studied these faces for as long as she can remember. She has encountered them in different forms, sometimes in the stones of old buildings, or glimpsed faintly in the reflection of a river.

They're part of an unseen world that has lived alongside with us for ages, a silent presence that has been in our world.

What is their purpose? She doesn't know for sure. But she senses there's an agenda behind their watching, some unspoken motive they guard closely.

Her assumption is that they are here to correct something, watch over some being, or maybe even engage in a fight with other similar creatures and some may be here for just entertainment.

This is not a mere fascination or hobby for her. This is everything to her. It has also become her identity.

This is what she does for a living. She is 'Trina the Face Trapper.'

She captures the essence of her encounters in photographs, each image carefully framed and mounted as a striking wall décor.

These aren't your average snapshots; they're haunting, some inspiring, emotional, dramatic, magnetic pieces of art that pulls you into another world.

She sells them at a decent price, and sometimes, when a particular piece resonates, bids come in unexpectedly high, and they all want it, the one that holds the magic.

Photographs aren't her only medium. She also seeks out objects with hidden faces—a rock with a faint outline, a wooden beam with eyes that seem to peer back, or an old weathered trunk that hides a sly grin in its grain.

Once she finds these objects, she polishes and restores them. These items, once silent and ordinary, are transformed under her care into enchanting, almost mystical artifacts.

How does someone buy them? Trina puts them out on her online store, describing the face, a story. A buyer has to see the face and it should connect to them. Once the buyer feels that this is a piece that 'I must have!', then Trina sells it to them.

For Trina, this is far more than a simple act of collecting and selling. Each piece she offers to her clients carries a story, and she weaves these tales from hours spent observing the faces.

One could argue that it's all her imagination or one could go by what she claims, 'that the story truly emerges, as if revealed to her by the object itself.'

To her clients, these stories are more than just background; they feel as though each piece connects them to another world, a hidden realm that seems to pulse with a life of its own.

Her clients are drawn to the mystery of these magical pieces, often feeling an inexplicable pull toward certain faces or forms. They tell her that these objects give them a sense of connection to something beyond the everyday—a world they can't fully understand but somehow feel.

It all began when she was seven.

Not exactly an age when they are taken seriously. Normally you'd brush it off if a child claimed to see a face somewhere.

But in the case of Trina, all of this crazy journey began on her birthday, as she was about to dive into the cake her mother had baked.

Friends and family were gathered, singing, and celebrating. The cake was sliced and shared, and as she looked down at her piece, she noticed something strange—a face in one of the cut sections.

She told her mother, who gently moved the slice to the kitchen. Word quickly spread, and everyone wanted to catch a glimpse. Most of them saw it too, and a few kids even nibbled a bit of the piece with the face.

Her uncle, who hadn't gotten a slice, joked, "since there is no more cake left and I am too hungry for a piece, this face must go down" and he devoured the piece.

At the time, she felt a little annoyed by that. But later, she thought—if she hadn't noticed the face, someone would have eaten it anyway.

From then on, she became curious, finding faces in all sorts of objects and creating stories about each one. Everybody around her enjoyed it.

They loved listening to these stories and her friends wanted to buy these objects. They all felt special buying these mysterious pieces.

She started to sell them, and it almost became her business. She started in school, and continued through her college, and eventually, her work became so popular that her parents, even though they found the business a bit odd, went along with her ideas and creations.

After all, it was bringing in good money. They also kept some of her collections at their home.

Her brother Daniel was not in approval of any of this. He felt she had to get out of this whole 'face thing' and have a life.

He would tell them that she was living in an illusion, which he thought had already gone too far.

To him, this was simply a case of face pareidolia—the mind's tendency to see faces in random patterns.

Face pareidolia is a fascinating psychological phenomenon where people perceive faces in random or inanimate objects. They would be able to see a 'face' in clouds, on a tree, or even in everyday items like toast or a piece of fruit.

This happens because our brain is wired to recognize faces quickly. One could say it as an evolutionary trait necessary for social bonding and survival.

We may need only minimal facial features—like some visible marks on the object for us to interpret them as a face, even if no real face is present.

But would Trina listen to any of this? Absolutely not.

She continued her journey until something strange began to unfold in her life.

As she got back from the park that evening, she went into her room. Her bedroom had some very special faces.

One was a giant rock, and it had the image of a lady, that she felt was here to find a child. The lady found solace in the human world watching us grow and bloom and have a good life.

There was a framed shot of a beach, and the whole picture was a giant face, probably an adventurous fellow who never wanted to confine into a single small object.

There were many other pictures and objects in her room and in her house, every single piece was special for Trina.

She jumped on to her bed and laid down for some time and that sometime drifted into a two-hour sleep.

When she got up, she was hungry, so she quickly made a sandwich with whatever she could find in her fridge and gobbled it up with some orange juice.

The she went to check the picture that she had taken.

She was shocked to see that the face wasn't there.

How is it possible?

She had carefully captured the face.

She has done it so many times. It cannot be an error.

Also, it is just not one shot. None of the pictures had the face. Like the face chose to walk away.

Her mind raced with many questions. Has she lost the talents? Her skill to see the faces or is it a warning?

Then she confirmed in her heart, it must be their deed; they must have caused this. The creatures must have come together and decided to put an end to her powers. She was beginning to get paranoid.

She called her brother.

"I can't see the face. I took the picture, I came back, and I am looking at it, and I can't see the face."

"Cool. Sounds good." He said in a way that meant she was finally on her path to recovery.

"Seriously, I am freaking out." She cried.

"Listen, why are you freaking out? None of us freaked out so much when we kept hearing over and over again about your faces!"

"You did."

"Yes, I did." Daniel agreed. "Of course... because I don't want you to attach to something that's not real and live in a fantasy world. I don't mind if it's just a hobby, but you are into it too much."

"Are you happy now that I lost the skill." Trina was losing her mind.

"What do you want me to do? I am sure it has happened before."

"No! It has never happened before."

"Why don't you go to the same place tomorrow and see if you can spot the face."

That was the best idea that he could suggest to her at that time. He had already begun to feel sleepy.

"Yeah, I guess I am going to do that." She hung up the phone.

Next day, Trina went to the park and stood in front of the same tree.

The face was missing. 'Anyway, I will let it pass' she thought even though deep inside she felt something strange about the whole thing.

Days passed by and she began seeing faces again and she took pictures, collected the objects and she continued what she was doing.

One day, as she was in a lonely place, a forest of a sort, she was walking, looking at everything around her and she had this deep desire to be the creature watching the world.

What if she could merge into something and experience what the creatures did.

What if by doing that she would know what this was all about.

So, she walked deep into the woods and never returned.

The missing of Trina was not something the family could ever come in terms with. She had disappeared. And they searched for her as much as they could.

They could now only hope that she was alive somewhere, even if it was in her mysterious world.

They were devastated and overwhelmed with guilt. They had never truly guided her, letting her wander freely, lost in the make-believe world she'd crafted for herself.

Daniel felt the heaviest burden of all.

He had seen her slipping away, sensed her danger, but never found the words to make her understand.

He had tried—but never hard enough, never with the urgency that might have saved his little sister.

How do you help the ones you love when no one seems to understand?

How many times should you try before giving up?

What can you do when someone is slipping away?

Daniel stood in her empty apartment, staring at the world she'd left behind. It was beautiful, whatever it was, it was unique. If these creatures are real, they better help he thought.

It may sound absurd but when there is nowhere else to turn, you turn to whatever you can.

And that's why Daniel decided to connect with the creatures.

He started looking at all the faces. The one that he could connect to. The face that was willing to help.

Then he saw the giant rock and the lady. The story of her yearning to have a child.

He looked at her and asked, "can you help me?"

"Are you there, will you help me?

You have been watching her, do you know where she is? Can you bring her back?"

He cried, broken.

Years passed by and Daniel built a life of his own. He married and had a daughter, whom he named after his lost sister.

When little Trina held a small rock from the beach and brought to her father claiming that she saw a face.

He looked it at closely and asked,

"What face do you see?"

"It's my aunts face," she claimed.

"Then it's very precious, you must keep it safe." His voice almost broken as he spoke.

At home he watched it carefully and asked, "is it you?

Is it you Trina?"

Next day, someone was at the door.

Thirteen years after she had vanished, his sister stood there; smiling as if she'd never left. The family was stunned.

Nobody knew what to say to her. She had left them broken.

Her parents rushed to Daniel's house to meet her. They could not believe that she was back, all they wanted was just to hug her and make sure everything was fine.

"I'm so sorry for hurting you all," she said.

The mother could not hold back, and she rushed with her question?

"Where were you my child, she sobbed. To where did you disappear?"

"Would you believe if I told you?"
Trina asked.

Everyone looked at her silently.

"You will not, right?" She asked looking at her family, expecting an answer.

"I will," Her niece said aloud.

"I will too," Daniel said.

"I will my child, I will." the mother cried.

"I will listen," the father said.

Daniel's wife smiled, "can I hear and then decide?"

"You poor thing must be so freaked out to see me." Trina said to her.

"You have no idea how happy and relieved we are to see you. Nothing else matters and you should know" she said giving her a hug.

Trina sat down comfortably on a chair, and they all sat around her, and she spoke, and they all listened.

"When I was there, I was watching this world, our beautiful world, it had special hue of colours and vibrations and emotions. It is so alive.

Also, all those objects that I have collected don't actually have any creatures in them. It's a shadow. If they have merged with anything, it casts a shadow of their face but that does not mean they are there.

They will never live in anything for long."

"Who are they? Daniel enquired. "Do they belong to our world?"

"They are part of this world."

"Are they here to take care of us or to trap us?" Little Trina asked.

"Don't trap them and they won't trap you."

"Did you ever trap them?" she asked again.

"I was known as the face trapper," she said and laughed.

Everyone laughed too and effortlessly they all slipped into their regular life.

In that little world of a few people, they all decided to be together. They decided to laugh, love and accept.

They did not know how to make sense of whatever happened. They felt it was not necessary. She was back and that was all that was important and that is all that matters.

Her world is for her to keep and enjoy and be a part of it whether it is real or not.

Who can be sure what is real and unreal?

What stories are true and what stories are not, who can prove?

Aren't we all trapped in our own versions of reality?

When someone very dear to you takes a path that you don't understand or you firmly believe is not good for them, you try with all your knowledge and power to help them, and yet you feel absolutely helpless having made no impact at all. At this point, you may choose to retrieve, stop or give up.

We are all in a little small box of our created reality, we can only do so much. Be kind to yourself and remember that others must walk their own paths, it is their journey too.

This story is for you, trying to make sense of what's happening, trying to save a dear one from those unknown paths they've chosen, for those who have lost dear ones in their struggles, and for the ones who are still waiting for their loved one's return.

Stay strong, Rose Butterfly

About The Author

Rose Butterfly is a pen name of Deena Philip, an Australian writer and publisher, best known for her profoundly empathetic self-help guide, ***The Book I Never Had.***

The book helps navigate heartbreaks and the lingering emotions of past relationships, providing readers with practical guidance. The work has resonated with many due to its relatable and understanding approach to emotional healing. She has also published a second edition to further answer her readers' questions.

Her work spans across different genres, and her versatile writing caters to both children and adults. She holds a Degree in **Media & Communications and Psychology,** and her work reflects a deep understanding of minds, relationships, philosophy and the human experience. She is also a theatre performer and an artist.

Her teen novel, ***Laser Boy and Ice Girl,*** is a thrilling sci-fi superhero comedy series for teens, while the ***Izzy and Mia*** collection, co-authored with **Avia Ranjith**, is a light and fun chapter book for younger readers.

Heart-Stirring Moments is a collection of short, introspective stories of life, its nuances, and moments. ***Imperfect Minds*** is volume two of the same collection.

Deena is also the head of the production house **'Cheer,'** which is involved in multiple creative projects.

www. cheerproductions.com.au

Visit the website to know more about the Author and other works.

www. rosebutterfly.com.au

Follow the Rose Butterfly Page on Facebook

Want to leave a review?

If you loved these stories and want to help others discover the book, write a review on the platform you purchased this book from.

You can also check out other books by the same author.
A collection of heart stirring and introspective stories of life, its nuances, and moments.

Heart stirring Moments written by **Rose Butterfly** is a collection of short stories that delicately weaves together emotions and indefinable feelings.

The book contains themes of love, unconventional relationships, courage, self-image, walking away, brokenness, letting go and healing. This Book is also designed as a '**Book to Gift'** with a dedicated page for you to write your message when gifting to someone dear, someone who loves stories.

Available on Amazon to Purchase

The Book I Never Had guides you in reclaiming your strength and moving forward from the pain and struggles of a breakup.

Available for purchase on Amazon

You need solid advice.
You need affirmations.
You need faith in life.
You need a guide.
The Book I Never Had has it all.
~Goodreads

"Whatever you may be going through in your relationship, if this book finds you, let there be something solely for you to embrace and discover. Let not your crisis shatter you, may you be able to navigate through it all with ease and emerge out in your true power."

Rose Butterfly

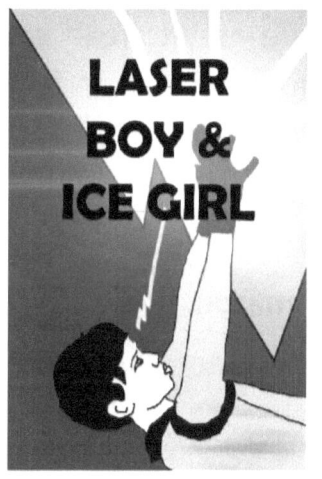 

Enjoy this action-packed sci-fi comedy, **'Laser Boy & Ice Girl- Volume 1 & 2.'** It is the ultimate genre mashup, blending action, humour, and suspense into a Kapow-worthy moments that you wouldn't want to miss.

- Perfect read for tweens, teens and young adults.

- Perfect choice for lovers of space and science fiction.

- Perfect book for comedy connoisseurs.

Available for purchase on Amazon

Izzy and Mia story books are easy-to-read chapter books, with friendship-based tales perfect for children who enjoy fun stories, naughty and silly moments of their day and tiny little adventures of life.

Available for purchase on Amazon.

www.ingramcontent.com/pod-product-compliance
Lightning Source LLC
Chambersburg PA
CBHW032001010726
47493CB00007B/2278